Moon Lake Loon Lake

Where Only The Elders Go

WHERE ONLY THE ELDERS GO
Moon Lake Loon Lake

Story by Jan Bourdeau Waboose

Watercolours by Halina Below

PENUMBRA PRESS

Published by PENUMBRA PRESS. Printed and bound in Canada.

CANADIAN CATALOGUING IN PUBLICATION DATA

Waboose, Jan Bourdeau
        Where only the elders go — Moon Lake Loon Lake / story by
Jan Bourdeau Waboose ; watercolours by Halina Below. — 2nd ed.
ISBN 1-894131-46-0
        1. Ojibwa Indians—Juvenile fiction. I. Below, Halina II. Title.
PS8595.A26W44 2003   jC813'.54   C2003-903250-7   PZ7

The publisher gratefully acknowledges the Canada Council for the Arts and the Ontario Arts Council for supporting Penumbra Press's publishing programme. The publisher further acknowledges the financial support of the Government of Canada through the Book Publishing Industry Development Program (BPIDP) for our publishing activities. We also acknowledge the Government of Ontario through the Ontario Media Development Corporation's Ontario Book Initiative.

Visit our website for other high quality books: www.penumbrapress.com

I wish to acknowledge Anishinabek Elders, Chiefs, and grassroots people who have inspired me throughout the years. I also wish to thank Halina Below for her never-ending encouragement.

— Meegwetch, *J.B.W.*

For my father, Timofey Below, remembered with love.

— *H.B.*

Introduction

This is a story of an Ojibway boy who hears the call of a Loon. It brings him memories of Mishomis.

Native Indians are joined in spirit with Mother Earth and respect all that she provides.

In this instance, Nature provides a mystic northern lake known as Moon Lake Loon Lake.

The Loon is a bird of many Indian legends. Mishomis is the Ojibway word for 'grandfather.'

An Ojibway boy hears the call of the Loon. He knows it is the bird of Indian legends.

He hears the Loon's cry again. He sits down beside the rippling water and stares into it. He remembers the story of long ago — a place where only the Elders go, Moon Lake Loon Lake.

During that distant time, in a distant forest, lies a remote northern lake where only the Elders go, Moon Lake Loon Lake.

The moon radiates light, and the stars glow in the calm still night.

The moon casts night shadows onto the dark, glassy water of the majestic birds where only the Elders go, Moon Lake Loon Lake.

Tall ancient trees entwine their branches sheltering the sacred place.

Except for the soft dipping of a wing rippling the water, it is tranquil.

It is a peaceful, restful place where only the Elders go, Moon Lake Loon Lake.

The wise Elder approaches, treading on soft moccasin feet. Quiet footsteps signal his presence to the graceful birds in their watery retreat.

Suddenly, the air is filled with a powerful stillness. He listens. In the distance he hears the haunting wail, the hypnotic call of the old Loon echoing across the lake.

It is mystical bird, the bird of Indian Legends. Where only the Elders go, Moon Lake Loon Lake.

The wise Elder sits down.

It is a time to think, a time to listen, a time to remember. He closes his eyes and sees a young boy running, laughing, learning.

He sees a man, a Chief, full of strength and spirit, and knowledge gained from his elders through time.

He opens his eyes and sees a man who has passed through time, who has learned wisdom, who has practised wisdom and shared his wisdom well.

And now it is time for him to leave it behind and move on, as the Loon leaves her offspring when they have learned all that she can give.

The Elder looks upon the shimmering lake and a smile comes across his face. He is surrounded by nature and feels life all around him. From the still, still waters he can see his breath against the night mist rise up like a cloud to the sky. It is getting colder, and he draws his body closer.

He looks up.

Suddenly, above him — a flash of white and black and grey, the colour of ashes — SWOOSH … SWOOSH … the beating of wings and feathers glistening in the moonlight.

Coming closer, closer, as silent as a shadow … the velvet throat calls out to him in a low voice. A calm, soft sound … a mellow song in the Elder's ears. It whispers like a dream.

The Elder lies down and closes his eyes. He lets his spirit go, peacefully. Where only the Elders go, Moon Lake Loon Lake.

The Ojibway boy again hears the call of the Loon. He sees the bird's shadow move quickly across the rippling water.

He looks up, but it is gone — the bird of Indian legends.

A smile comes across his face.

He is surrounded by nature.

He feels life all around him.

He is filled with love for Mishomis and remembers the stories he told of long ago — where only the Elders go, Moon Lake Loon Lake.

JAN BOURDEAU WABOOSE, a Nishnawbe Ojibway, grew up in northern Ontario. She began writing poetry and stories as a young child. For many years she worked with First Nations political associations, specializing in Education and Child Welfare programs. Her writing has appeared in magazines, newspapers and anthologies. Among Jan's award winning published works are *Morning on the Lake* (Kids Can Press), *Skysisters* (Kids Can Press) and *Firedancers* (Stoddart Publishing). Jan's writing reflects her respect and love for our natural surroundings and her people's traditions.

HALINA BELOW was born in Germany of Russian and Ukrainian parents and immigrated to Canada when she was two years old. Halina is also the author of *The Windy Day* (Lester, 1994), the illustrator of *The Best Gifts* (Fitzhenry & Whiteside, 1998) and *Just Imagine* (Fitzhenry & Whiteside, 1998), and both the author and illustrator of *Chestnut Dreams* (Fitzhenry & Whiteside, 2000).

OTHER FIRST NATIONS STORIES FOR CHILDREN BY PENUMBRA PRESS

ANYTIME STORIES

Leo Sawicki
Illustrated by
Michael Robinson
ISBN 0920806783
Softcover, $9.95
A collection of ten stories about Native children and their experiences. Many of the stories revolve around children learning to solve a problem or discovering their own resources in a time of difficulty.

ANYWHERE STORIES

Leo Sawicki
Illustrated by
Leo Neilson
ISBN 0921254474
Softcover, $9.95
This collection of short stories is drawn from many tribes, customs and ceremonies of the North American Indian. The purpose of these stories is to heighten our consciousness of how they are told, and ignite their imaginations.

NANNA BIJOU:
THE SLEEPING GIANT
Jocelyne Villeneuve
Illustrated by
Luc Robert
ISBN 0920806260
Softcover, $6.95
Nowadays, in a panoramic view never to be forgotten, one can see the gigantic figure of Nanna Bijou, a great land formation outlined in the bay of Lake Superior. So popular it has been reprinted three times!

GREENMANTLE:
AN OJIBWAY LEGEND OF THE NORTH
Jocelyne Villeneuve
Illustrated by
Luc Robert
ISBN 0921254520
Softcover, $9.95
An ancient love story set in the wild and romantic northland. This present-tense narrative tells of the beautiful Greenmantle, the only daughter of Ogama Eagle, the mighty Chief of the vast Algoma domain.

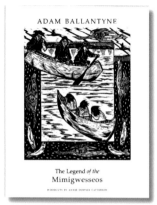

THE LEGEND OF
THE MIMIGWESSEOS
Adam Ballantyne
Illustrated by
Annie Downes
Catterson
ISBN 0921254806
Softcover, $9.95
The Mimigwesseos
lived among rocks
on islands and in
the ledges and cliffs
of lakes and rivers;
elf-like creatures with flat, noseless faces, they were
sometimes helpful but were dangerous to meddle
with. This book is about them.

WISAKYJAK
AND THE NEW
WORLD
Adam Ballantyne
Illustrated by
Annie Downes
Catterson
ISBN 0921254342
Softcover, $9.95
Wisakyjak is one of
the many characters
within the spiritual
world of the Wood-
land Cree Indians of Northern Canada. A trickster as
well as a friend, Wisakyjak can change the appearance
and form of many creatures.

TO ORDER BOOKS FROM PENUMBRA PRESS, please fill out this order form and send it with your cheque or money order to:

Penumbra Press, P O Box 940, Manotick, ON Canada K4M 1A8. Orders will be filled promptly.

Name _____

Address _____

_____

Phone _____

For accurate prices and delivery options please refer to www.penumbrapress.com
or call 1-613-692-5590. GST 103938023.

☐ Anytime Stories, $9.95
☐ Anywhere Stories, $9.95
☐ Nanna Bijou: The Sleeping Giant, $6.95
☐ Greenmantle: An Ojibway Legend of the North, $9.95
☐ The Legend of the Mimigwesseos, $9.95
☐ Wisakyjak and the New World, $9.95